DR XARGLE'S
BOOK OF
EARTHLETS

DR XARGLE'S
BOOK OF
EARTHLETS

A Red Fox Book

Published by Random House Children's Books
20 Vauxhall Bridge Road, London SW1V 2SA

A division of Random House UK Ltd
London Melbourne Sydney Auckland
Johannesburg and agencies throughout the world

First published by Andersen Press 1988
Red Fox edition 1990

9 10

Printed in Hong Kong

RANDOM HOUSE UK Limited Reg. No. 954009

ISBN 0 09 964010 4

DR XARGLE'S
BOOK OF
EARTHLETS

Translated into Human by Jeanne Willis
Pictures by Tony Ross

RED FOX

Good morning, class.

Today we are going to learn about Earthlets.

They come in four colours. Pink, brown, black or
yellow ... but not green.

They have one head and only two eyes, two short tentacles with pheelers on the end and two long tentacles called leggies.

They have square claws which they use to frighten off
wild beasts known as Tibbles and Marmaduke.

Earthlets grow fur on their heads but not enough to keep them warm.

They must be wrapped in the hairdo of a sheep.

Very old Earthlings (or "Grannies") unravel the sheep
and with two pointed sticks they make Earthlet
wrappers in blue and white and pink.

Earthlets have no fangs at birth.
For many days they drink only milk through a hole in
their face.

When they have finished the milk they must be patted and squeezed to stop them exploding.

When they grow a fang, the parent Earthling takes
the egg of a hen and mangles it with a prong.

Then she puts the eggmangle on a small spade and tips it into the Earthlet's mouth, nose and ears.

To stop them leaking, Earthlets must be pulled up by
the back tentacles and folded in half.
Then they must be wrapped quickly in a fluffy triangle
or sealed with paper and glue.

During the day, Earthlets collect the hairs of Tibbles
and Marmaduke, mud, eggmangle and banana.

They are then placed in plastic capsules with warm water and a yellow floating bird.

After soaking, Earthlets must be dried carefully to
stop them shrinking.
Then they are sprinkled with dust to stop them
sticking to things.

Earthlets can be recognised by their fierce cry,
"WAAAAAAA!"

To stop them doing this, the Earthling daddy picks
them up and flings them into the atmosphere.

Then he tries to catch them.

If they still cry, the Earthling mummy pulls their pheelers one by one and says "This little piggy went to market" until the Earthlet makes a "hee hee" noise.

If they still cry, they are sent to a place called
beddybyes.

This is a swinging box with a soft lining in which
there lives a small bear called Teddy.

That is the end of today's lesson.

If you are all very good and quiet we are going to put
our disguises on and visit planet Earth to see some
real Earthlets.

The spaceship leaves in five minutes.